MURDER ON AUTOPILOT

NIKI DUPRE SHORT STORIES BOOK 3

JIM RILEY

CHAPTER ONE

"COME ON, Mom. I don't want to look like a nun," Jamie Martin pleaded.

The teenager celebrated her sixteenth birthday the day before. Her biggest present was the car she was now driving. Not really driving. It was the automobile industry's industry's newest technology, a virgin model of the Eagle Autocar, able to drive without human intervention.

Jamie planned to spend some of the money she received from her grandmother on a silk low–cotton blouse that would accentuate her perky top. Andy Netterville, the captain of the football team, was the target of her affection. The two teenagers had dated for three months, and he was a full–blooded high testosterone athlete. So far, she had resisted his aggressive advances. But tonight would be the special time for them to consummate their relationship, her first time with any young man.

Jamie planned to go alone to the Mall of Louisiana, but her mom insisted on going along. Lois Martin had never ridden in a self–directed automobile and was nervous with her husband's choice. Ralph Martin's reasoned the car would be safer, driving itself instead of in the teenager's hands. His daughter was no different from most, totally absorbed in constant contact with her friends on her iPhone.

"I don't want you to wear something that would give that young man the wrong idea," Lois answered her daughter.

The teenager turned to face her mother, letting the automobile navigate itself through the traffic on Interstate 12 from Denham Springs.

"Mom, I'm almost an adult. Why can't you trust me?"

"I trust you, honey. But I don't trust football players. I dated a few of them in my day."

"How did you dress for your dates?" Jamie asked.

"We're not talking about me. It's your future I'm concerned about."

Jamie had already determined she would buy two tops, one to show her mom, and the silk one to wear on the date. She also wanted some form-fitting jeans a half size too small. Although she did not think it was necessary to excite Andy further, she wanted him filled with desire for her.

They passed the Amite River bridge, and the car increased in speed to the limit with no effort on Jamie's part. She loved the car. She could text, listen to music, and talk to her friends in it without the worry of other traffic. It was a teenager's dream.

Then the car eased up another ten miles per hour.

"Mom, it's speeding. I don't want to get a ticket on my first ride in it. What should I do?"

"Tap the brakes," Lois answered. "According to the manual, that will let you take control back."

Jamie lightly stepped on the brake. The car sped up another ten miles per hour. Then she stomped on the brake. The car continued going eighty miles an hour. Even at this speed, the auto control expertly maneuvered through the light traffic on a Saturday morning.

"Let me call your father," Lois jerked her cell phone out of her purse.

"I don't know what to do," Jamie's eyes widened with fright.

Joe did not answer his cell, an occurrence that happened all too often to suit Lois. She did not leave a message, slamming the phone back in her purse. When she looked up, the mother could not believe how many cars they were passing.

At the Sherwood Forest exit, the car was going ninety miles per hour. A mile later, at the Airline Highway exit, it was up to ninety–five. Still skillfully dodging all the other traffic, the automobile reached a hundred miles per hour at the I–10 junction.

Jamie screamed when they left the main road and rode on the shoulder of the interstate. Lois tried to do something, but in her panic, she froze.

At the College Drive exit, they sped at a hundred ten miles per hour. The number of lanes tightened from four to three, further congesting the mass of travelers.

The auto car clipped the back of a semi-truck and spun. Both females found their voices, letting out shrills that could be heard above the traffic's din.

Jamie's car crashed through the cement retainer above College Avenue. Lois and Jamie felt the hand of death approaching. The teenager knew she would never consummate her relationship with Andy. Her final thought was what she had missed.

The car went through the retainer and landed twenty feet below in the bed of a pickup. Lois and Jamie did not feel the impact. They were no longer feeling anything.

CHAPTER TWO

Lyle Houston paced back and forth. He was way too jazzed to sit. The future of his whole company was a stake. His entire future was in jeopardy. Lyle owned eighty percent of Eagle Autocar. Ralph Smith owned the other twenty percent.

CNN, Fox News, MSNBC, and all the major networks were rebroadcasting the Eagle Autocar Sparrow crash against the concrete blockades. A motorist, seeing the automatic car speed by, filmed it with her smartphone. It went viral and made international news. The whole world viewed the incident.

The customers stayed away in droves, except for those who wanted to return their Sparrows. His sales staff had to assure each one the crash was an anomaly. They tried to assure them they were in no danger of the same happening to their cars.

But that was okay because no new customers were standing in line to get a chance to purchase a new electric Sparrow. Before the deaths of Lois and Jamie Martin, people could not wait for the usual six months to receive the delivery.

Almost a quarter of those had already called and told the unfortunate salesmen where they could stuff the deposit.

The company was not cash affluent. Lyle borrowed against future sales, putting the financial health of Eagle Autocar in peril. Houston had already invested his entire life savings. Plus, he had put a second mortgage on his home he shared with his wife and three daughters. All three of the girls were in their teens as if Lyle did not have enough distractions.

After wearing a hole in the carpet behind his desk, Lyle did the only thing he thought of that might help. The automobile company owner picked up the desk phone and dialed the number of the most famous private investigator in Louisiana. He started talking as soon as Niki Dupre picked up.

CHAPTER THREE

LYLE STILL PACED after Niki arrived in his office. The long-legged detective sat calmly on the other side of the huge cherry desk. The owner had already smoked three cigarettes and was lighting a fourth while describing the situation to her. While he paced, ht also lit the fourth cancer stick. Niki asked a question.

"How do you know it's not a design flaw?"

"Because we don't have any flaws in our design," Lyle responded. Ralph and I were the designers. We made no mistakes."

"Who is Ralph? Does he still work for Eagle Autocar?"

"No, he doesn't. Ralph and I started the company based on an idea we had sitting in a bass boat one day. He wasn't as wealthy, so I put it up all the money, and he brought his tremendous skills to the partnership. But he is no longer active."

"Why not?" Niki asked. "If I owned twenty percent of an internationally known company, I'd be here every minute of every day."

"We had a minor disagreement. Not over the automated features of our design, but on other matters." Lyle answered.

"How disgruntled is Ralph? Would he go as far as sabotaging a car to settle the argument?"

Lyle stopped pacing. He stuffed the four cigarettes in an ashtray and lit the fifth one. At this rate, Niki felt he would easily go through an entire carton in one day.

CHAPTER FOUR

"Is THERE anyone else upset with you and the company?" Niki asked. "Competitors? Employees? Customers?"

"One competitor," Lyle replied. "Rufus Pruitt. He accused Ralph and me of stealing the design from him. He filed a lawsuit with the East Baton Rouge Parish courts."

"Is there any basis for his claim?" Niki asked.

Lyle stalled and lit another cigarette, even though the fifth one was only half-smoked. "We might've borrowed some of his concepts, but none were copyrighted."

"Will he win in court?" Niki asked.

"It doesn't look like it. If Rufus had taken the time and spent the money to register his concepts, it would be a different story. But so far, every ruling we have had has been to our advantage, not his."

"Did he seem upset with you?"

Lyle laughed, his oversize belly shaking up and down. "If you call throwing a punch at me as upset, then I guess he was."

"How long ago did this happen? What did you do?"

"It happened two days before the Sparrow crashed. Right on the courthouse steps. I pressed assault charges against Rufus."

"That had to piss him off even more," Niki said. "Did he say anything that would make you think he was involved?"

"He told me I would not enjoy one red cent from his invention. He said he would never let it happen."

CHAPTER FIVE

"Suppose Rufus or someone else wanted to sabotage your automated systems. How difficult would it be?" Niki asked.

"Impossible," Lyle answered. "Somebody could break into the Pentagon easier than getting into ours. We took great pains to implement every security feature known to man."

"What is the possibility of a defective chip? Could the one you put into Martin's car have gone awry somewhere?"

"Come on, I'll show you why that isn't realistic."

Lyle charged out of the room. Niki had to use her long legs to catch up with the agitated owner. He was like a Whitetail buck during the rut. He had one thing on his mind. The only difference was Lyle wasn't thinking about sex. He wanted to find a way to put his life back on track.

Niki followed Lyle through a maze of hallways. People in the offices were getting little work done. Instead, they clustered in groups of three or four. As soon as they saw Lyle, the men and women broke up, only reassembling as soon as the boss passed by. There would be no productivity today.

They entered a room that appeared to be a laboratory rather than an office. Rows and rows of computer monitors sat on the wall. There were no partitions. The men and women, mostly men, sitting in front of the monitors were completely engaged with the data flowing across the screen. Not one bothered to look up at Lyle.

"This is the brains of our company. Every one of these people is an expert in his or her field. They are the very best money can buy. This is our biggest investment in the entire company."

"I'm a little out of my league here. Computer technology is not my forte, but I know someone that can talk to your people intelligently. Do you mind if I call her?"

CHAPTER SIX

EVEN AMONG A BUNCH of computer geeks, Donna Cross turned heads. The hourglass blonde caught the attention of every male in the room and some of the females. The once enthralling data was now being ignored among whispers that grew like a spreading storm. Soon, every eye was trained on Donna's perfectly symmetrical body.

"Donna," Niki said, ignoring the stairs. "This is Lyle Houston. He is the majority owner of Eagle Autocar."

"Hi," Donna responded to the chubby man with a cigarette dangling from his mouth. Lyle completely forgot about it as soon as Niki's business partner entered the room.

Lyle straightened his tie and brushed the ashes off his shirt before extending a hand to the vivacious young lady.

"Hi–are you a computer expert? You don't look like any of them I've ever interviewed," he rasped.

"Don't let looks fool you," Niki laughed. "Although your productivity in this room is nonexistent since she arrived."

"Back to work, everybody," he shouted. "This ain't no peepshow."

"Who is the best person to talk to to get some straight answers?" Donna asked. "I need facts, no BS."

"Uh–That would be Dennis. Dennis Walker," Lyle said. "He's our lead design engineer. He knows everything about the Sparrow."

CHAPTER SEVEN

IF NIKI HAD LOOKED up a nerd definition on Google, Dennis Walker's picture would have popped up. His hair was slicked back with an inordinate amount of grease. He wore striped slacks and a striped shirt that did not match.

Dennis had a plastic pocket protector in one of the two pockets on his shirt. It was crammed full of pens, pencils, and small calligraphic utensils. When he saw Donna headed his way with Lyle and Niki, the engineer almost fell out of his chair.

"Dennis," Lyle said. "This is Donna Cross. She has a few questions about our security protocols. I'm sure you can explain it in a language she can understand."

Donna stuck her hand out toward Dennis. "Hi there."

Dennis seemed unsure of what to do. He stared at Donna's hand like it was a serpent. Then Donna completely baffled him. She reached over and gave him a peck on his cheek. It might as well have been right hook. Dennis fell back in his chair with such a force it almost flipped over backward.

"Eagle Autocar is a great place to work in. We attract only the best and the brightest," Lyle grinned before he caught a glimpse of Niki's face. "Unfortunately, we have no openings today."

"That's okay. I will never leave Niki," Donna said. "Without her, I would make so many mistakes, I'd never get past them."

"What did you find out about the system?" Niki asked. "Is there any way anyone could back into it?"

"A kindergartner with a smartphone," Donna laughed. "It might take thirty minutes if he was eating Cracker Jacks."

"I can't believe that," Lyle spurted out. "We have the best minds in America. Nobody can penetrate our system."

"I beg to differ, Lyle," Donna said sweetly. "I believe I can prove you wrong if given a chance."

"I'm willing to bet a thousand dollars you can't get into our system. The hell with thirty minutes. I'll give you twenty-four hours or more. You still won't be able."

"I'll cover Donna's side of that," Niki said. "And she would prefer cash to a check, especially under the circumstances."

CHAPTER EIGHT

THE THREE WENT BACK to Lyle's office. There Niki sipped on a Dr. Pepper only because the vending machine did not carry cherry Dr. Pepper. Lyle opened a fresh pack of cigarettes despite disapproving looks from both Niki and Donna. Donna opened her laptop, and her delicate fingers flew across the keyboard too fast for either of the others to follow. After four minutes, Donna grinned.

After six, she said, "I'm ready if you guys are."

"Show me what you found, though I may not believe it," Lyle said. "I still believe in the integrity of our systems."

"Then it would be better if we went to the showroom. I believe I can demonstrate your network is vulnerable."

"Why the showroom?" Lyle asked. "Why not here?"

"Because you have no Sparrows in your office. I need at least one to make my point. Do you mind?"

Lyle stared at the hourglass blonde for a long time. He closed his eyes for several seconds. When he opened them, he said, "I don't believe it. Would you care to double the bet? I've got a good feeling you're pulling my leg."

Niki laughed. "I'll cover that also. Unlike you, I've seen that look on her face before. She's already in your system."

CHAPTER NINE

THE THREE OF them left the office and walked to the Eagle Autocar showroom. Lyle had a stern look. Niki was smiling. Donna boasted a huge grin.

"Let's go over to the blue one," Donna said as soon as they entered the expanse.

There was no customers in sight. It was as if they were all afraid of the plague. Even the few salesmen standing around were disinterested until they saw Donna from across the room. Their renewed interest had nothing to do with the integrity of the Sparrow systems.

When the trio got near the blue Sparrow, Donna bent over and read the VIN, or vehicle identification number.

"I'm doing this because I only want to affect one car in the demonstration. I could pick one at random you sold in your inventory, but let's stick with this one for now."

"Come on," Lyle said. "You can quit this right now. You really don't have to embarrass yourself anymore."

"I don't think I'll be the one embarrassed," Donna said. "When I get through, I think you'll agree with me instead."

"Then what are you waiting for?" Lyle asked. "Get after it."

Donna winked at Niki, then sat at one of the sales desks. Her fingers once again glided over the keyboard. Then the Sparrow's engine came to life.

"How–how did you do that? Did you steal one of our Eagle Autocar starters from the back? That must be it," Lyle said.

Donna's fingertips hit more keys. The blue Sparrow went forward about three feet. Then our lights flashed and then backed up the same three feet. Then the hood flew open. It was followed in less than two seconds by the trunk. After that, the driver's side door springs open. The alarm system sounded, and the horn flared.

Lyle felt like his body had been taken over by an alien. One that was not on the friendly side of life.

Donna just grinned, watching the Sparrow go through various gyrations.

CHAPTER TEN

"How DID YOU DO THAT?" Lyle asked, finally able to stammer.

"Actually, it was a bit harder than I thought," Donna said. "I thought I could get into your chip in two minutes. It took me four."

"But we have all of these protections. Where did you find a weakness in them?"

"Your technicians can do remote diagnosis as part of the upgraded features of the Sparrow. That way, the customers can find out what is wrong with the car before they bring it in."

"That's right," Lyle said. "Our customers love it. They can get the mechanics to fix the problem without further analysis."

"Your techs access the computer chips through the GPS system. As long as the GPS is on, they have access to the brains of the system."

"Correct," nodded Lyle. "That was the most efficient way. To directly access the chips would have been cost-prohibitive."

"Maybe so, but you left your entire system open to hackers. They have a boulevard to the control of your cars."

"What can we do? I can't have another incident like this one."

"Disconnect the GPS system until Dennis and the other engineers can figure out a workaround," Donna said.

"Do you know what that will do to our reputation?" Lyle asked.

"It will have less damage than a few more dead people," Niki said.

CHAPTER ELEVEN

THEY WERE INTERRUPTED by a noise rising from the lot. The noise rose to a din. Niki looked up to see a dozen people carrying signs and chanting. The small group tried to make up for their scarce numbers with a vociferous attack. They charged inside despite the protests of a few of the salesmen that still lingered.

Lyle stepped forward, more courageous than Niki had given him credit. The owner faced down the lead protester.

"This is private property. I must ask you to leave."

"So, you can keep making cars that kill people?" The protester said. "When did profits become more important than life?"

"The Sparrow is one of the safest cars on the American roads today," Lyle said. "We are proud of our safety record."

"But your smart cars are too smart," the protester said. "They can take complete control away from the driver."

"That's not true. We are investigating the incident and will submit reports to the proper authorities as soon as we complete them. I assure you we will find out what happened."

"We'll be here to make sure you don't sell any more of those death traps until you fix the problem," the protester replied.

"I'm sorry, but I can't allow you to do that. If you don't leave immediately, I'll have to call the police."

In response, the lead protester swung at Lyle. The sign's handle hit the owner on top of his head, sending him crashing to the floor. Then the protester raised the stake to hit him again. He never got the chance.

Niki's foot hit him in the upper sternum. She did not want to break any bones. She only wanted to prevent the man from continuing his assault on Lyle.

However, more of the protesters pressed forward, unable to control their agitated emotions. One came at Niki from her left side. She deflected the blow with an outside arm guard. Then the long-legged detective pounded a foot into the man's stomach, doubling him over and sending him to the floor.

Another came from her right side. Niki delivered a straight right jab to the man's nose. It was not a fatal blow, but it was strong enough to stop him.

Then the entire crowd erupted, all trying to get a piece of the strawberry blonde. They came at her from all directions.

CHAPTER TWELVE

"Looks like a mess," Samson Mayeaux said. He was the chief of homicide for the East Baton Rouge Sheriff's Department. He was also Niki's mentor and close friend. Samson and his wife took Niki when her parents were murdered when she was only sixteen years old. The murder was never solved.

He, Niki, and Donna stood to one side of the showroom, watching the EMTs administer treatment to the injured protesters. And there were many. Nine of the dozen were writhing on the floor with an assortment of injuries

"I had no choice, Samson," Niki said. "They attacked Lyle, and when I came to his defense, they attacked me."

"Don't worry about it, little girl," Samson used the pet name for the detective as he had since she was in diapers.

"I have to worry about it. Lyle hired me to protect him, and now I've brought a lot of bad publicity his way."

Samson laughed. "I imagine Mr. Houston sooner rather have a bit of adverse publicity rather than a cracked skull."

"Why does this always seemed to happen to me?" Niki sighed.

"Because you won't take whatever life dishes out. You like to cook your own meals."

CHAPTER THIRTEEN

RALPH SMITH WAS NOT who or what Niki expected. She was anticipating the electrical engineer to look like one, similar to Dennis Walker, back at the Eagle Autocar offices. Instead, she found an athletic man in his mid-thirties. His wavy, brown hair was accented with dark blue eyes and a natural tan. He carried the minimum body fat.

"So, you're trying to get Lyle out of a bind," he said. They sat beside his pool at a patio table.

"I wish I could tell you good luck, but I'd be lying if I did."

"Why don't you want Eagle Autocar to succeed? Niki asked. "I understand you still own twenty percent of the company."

"I do, only because I feel bad about dumping the stock on one of my friends. An enemy maybe, but not a friend."

"What caused the animosity between you and Lyle?" Niki asked.

"He's the third–rate engineer who won't listen to those around him who know what they're saying and doing," Ralph responded.

"Can you give me an example? One I can understand? I'm not the most proficient computer tech in the world."

"Sure. You know all the eco–nuts that think an electric car would save the earth from climate change? Correct?"

"Yes. Burning electricity is a lot cleaner than burning fossil fuels. Plus, electricity is able to be replicated. Once we use fossil fuels, they're gone for good."

"Where does electricity come from?" Ralph asked.

"Uh–you're getting out of my area of expertise, but I think it comes from the electrical plants or nuclear facilities."

"You're absolutely right. Let's address nuclear first. How many nuclear plants do you suppose supply electricity to Louisiana?"

"I know there is one up in St. Francisville," Niki said. "I'm not sure how many more we have in Louisiana."

"That's the only one. It supplies less than one percent of the entire electrical usage in our state. To put it bluntly, the nuclear industry has no impact on our energy needs."

"But we still have the electrical plants. They must be doing a good job because we've got plenty," Niki said.

"What do those plants use for fuel?" Ralph asked.

"I'm not sure. I know clean coal was making a comeback. I assume a lot of them have switched to natural gas since we seem to have a surplus of it lately."

"True. All the plants use some form of fossil fuels. No matter how clean coal ever gets, natural gas is so much better. And we have a surplus of natural gas for the foreseeable future. We are the Saudi Arabia of the world in those terms."

"So you didn't want the Sparrows to be electric? What did you want them to use instead?" Niki asked.

"Natural gas, of course. It's cheap. It's plentiful. It's clean-burning. It causes low stress on an engine. It's the perfect fuel."

"And Lyle wouldn't agree? Is that why you left?"

"No," Ralph responded. "There was a much bigger problem."

CHAPTER FOURTEEN

"I WARNED Lyle about the vulnerability of our network," Ralph said. "It was a disaster waiting to happen."

"Why wouldn't Lyle listen to you?" Niki asked.

"Two reasons," Ralph responded. "Time and money. Both were more important to Lyle than security."

"Can you expand?" Niki asked. "I want to get it straight."

"Let's address the money first. It would've cost us several million dollars to erect a firewall between the GPS system and the rest of the control executive files. Lyle didn't want or couldn't afford to spend that kind of money."

"Lyle gave me the impression he was unaware of the susceptibility of the gateway to the control chips," Niki said.

Ralph snorted. "He was aware of it. He and I argued about it for weeks. I have copies of the letters I sent him on the very subject. I guess he forgot to show you those."

"He didn't," she admitted, feeling much less confident in the man who hired her to find a solution to the case. If he was hiding the letters, what else could he be keeping secret? "Do you have copies of those letters?"

Ralph nodded. "I wanted protection from liability when it all hit the fan. I also have a release of liability signed by Lyle Houston himself. No way he can deny it."

"You mentioned time as well as money. Would it have taken longer to create a firewall?" Niki asked.

"More than Lyle was willing to wait for," Ralph responded.

"How much time are we talking about?"

"I guess you've heard about the three qualities the filling an order. *Good. Fast. Cheap.* You can pick two of those at any time, but never all three for one order. For a good system, we were looking at more than a year. That includes the design and testing and making corrections."

"Why didn't Lyle want to take the time?" Niki asked.

"Cash flow," answered Ralph. "He didn't have any. All of the venture capital went to Tesla and the big boys. Lyle was left looking for investors like me. But then he wouldn't listen to me."

"How close was Lyle to running out of money?"

"Maybe six months. Maybe a couple of more. Money was bleeding out and wasn't being replaced. We had to take the Sparrow to the market or sell the idea to someone else."

"Why didn't he do that? He could have taken the money and retired without all the headaches he has now," Niki said.

"Ego," Ralph responded. "Most entrepreneurs have a huge one, and Lyle Houston is no different. There was no way he would give up his concept for money."

"Is there anything else Lyle failed to tell me?" Niki asked.

"Did he tell you about the *interruption of services clause* he took out on his insurance policy?"

CHAPTER FIFTEEN

"WHAT IS AN *INTERRUPTION OF SERVICES CLAUSE*?" Niki asked. "I don't believe I've ever heard of that."

"The basic effect is the insurance company will pay a substantial sum of money to Eagle Autocar if we are temporarily put out of business through no fault of the company."

"But if there is a design flaw, wouldn't that be the fault of the company?" Niki asked, shaking her long strawberry blonde mane.

"If the insurance company can prove it," Ralph answered. "Why do you think you were hired?"

"To find out what went wrong so that Eagle Autocar could fix it and prevent another incident in the future."

"That would be the naïve perception," Ralph said, "My own is much more realistic than yours seems to be."

"And what is your perception of why Lyle hired me?"

"To see if the vulnerability was obvious. Since you found it on the first day of your investigation, I see it was."

"Well, I wouldn't murder two people just to generate cash flow from the insurance company. I don't believe that."

"Come on, Niki. People get killed for less than a hundred dollars in Baton Rouge every day. With Eagle Autocar, Lyle was looking at losing millions, if not billions."

CHAPTER SIXTEEN

JOE MARTIN LIVED in a less exclusive area of the Baton Rouge Metroplex. He lived across the Amite River in Denham Springs down Interstate 12. The two victims' husband and father were still at home, adjusting to life without his loved ones.

"Thank you for seeing me, Mr. Martin," Niki said after she was seated in his den. "This must be very difficult for you."

"Please call me Joe. I'm not that much older than you," he said.

"Okay, Joe. Do you mind talking about what happened?"

"I don't think it'll ever get any easier. They were my life. They was the reason I got up in the morning."

"I'm sorry for your loss. Are you sure I shouldn't come back at a later date? I really wouldn't mind."

"I'd rather get it over with," Joe said. "I don't want it hanging out there over my head. Are you representing Eagle Autocar?"

"They are my employer for this case. But like I told Lyle Houston, I will search for the truth no matter where that leads. If the accident was Eagle Autocar's fault, I'd report it."

"I don't plan to sue them," Joe shrugged. "I believe in God, and He is in control. He wanted my babies to be in heaven with Him."

"That's a great attitude. I'm not sure I could be so forgiving if I were to switch places with you," Niki said.

"It's really selfish," Joe said. "I want to remember Lois and Jamie and all the good times we had. I don't want a long, drawn-out trial about how they died."

"You've gained my respect. What made you buy a Sparrow for your daughter in the first place?"

"I'm a computer systems designer. I thought it was cool. I could buy a car that utilized the best technology in my chosen field. I felt comfortable with it."

"Was Jamie familiar with the features of the car?" Niki asked.

"I spent three hours going over them with her Friday night," he chuckled. "I doubt if she heard more than three minutes."

"I'm familiar with the attention span of teenagers," Niki said. "Or rather the lack of it in most cases."

"Jamie was a good girl, but she was a teenager. She was at the age where she thought Lois and I were old fogies."

"That's not unusual," Niki said. "Do you know of anyone who would want to harm either Lois or Jamie?"

"No way," Ralph shook his head. "Lois was a saint. She was the best friend I had. Everybody loved her from the instant they met her. She was that kind of person."

"What about Jamie?" Niki asked. "Was she having any troubles with the other kids in school? Any use of drugs?"

"No way. She was a cheerleader, and they get tested all the time. If she were doing any drugs, Lois and I would have known about it. I can assure you my daughter wasn't."

"Any trouble with the other kids? Was there any that she didn't get along with?"

"I don't think so. My girl was very popular. She was dating the starting quarterback. I guess some of the kids might have been jealous, but Jamie never said anything about it."

"How about the relationship between you and Jamie? Was it okay?"

"Better than okay. It was fabulous, better than I could have ever imagined."

"And the relationship between you and Lois? How was that?"

"It's simple," Joe smiled. "She was the love of my life. I worshiped the ground she walked on."

CHAPTER SEVENTEEN

Niki's next stop was at an engineering design shop office on Sherwood Forest, Bayou Blue Technologies. From the information Donna was able to garner from the web, Rufus Pruitt was the sole proprietor. He was the man that Lyle mentioned as a disgruntled competitor.

The outside of the building was maintained, and the lawn was well manicured with just enough shrubs and flowers. The inside looked as if a hurricane hit it. Electrical circuits, computer frames, loose wires, and spare parts were strewn on every surface.

There was no one at the front desk, which was covered with three cardboard boxes. An antenna leaned against one side. The chair behind it contained a sack full of parts.

"Hello," Niki called down the congested hallway. A small path wound through the equipment and gear stored all its length.

A head popped out an office. It's sported gray hair and lots of wrinkles. Thick glasses rested on top of his nose.

"Go away," he said. "I don't have time for more business."

"Are you Mr. Pruitt?" Niki asked while walking toward him.

"I already told you. I don't have time. I'm a busy man."

"Mr. Pruitt, I'm Niki Dupre. I'm investigating the incident where two people died in the crash of the Eagle Autocar Sparrow. I understand you had a hand in the original design."

By this time, Niki was almost next to the small man. He had to look up at the lean strawberry blonde.

"Oh, all right," he said. "Five minutes and no more."

Rufus Pruitt's office was a mirror image of the rest of the building. Even the guest chairs were covered with all sorts of packages and parts. Niki had no choice but to stand, making her tower over the small man after he sat down.

"Were you part of the original design?" She asked.

"I was more than that," Pruitt responded. "It was my design, and those thieves stole it right out from under me."

"I assume you're talking about Lyle Houston and Ralph Smith," Niki waited for Rufus to nod. "Lyle told me you never copyrighted your concepts."

"And why should I?" Pruitt yelled. "We had an agreement. All the designs would be registered to our corporation. The only thing is, it turned out to be his company. He left me completely out of it."

"How upset were you when he defaulted on the agreement?"

"If you mean when he stole the best idea I've ever had, I was more than mad. I would've killed him given a chance."

Niki had a hard time imagining this small man physically attacking anyone. However, he seemed perfectly capable of sabotaging one of Lyle Houston's scars. He had the temperament for it.

"Did you know of the vulnerability of the control chip in the design? Did you address the issue when you were involved?"

"Any idiot other than that thief would know it was a problem. If he had stuck to my design, he wouldn't be having the problems he's having now."

"Did your design offer more protection against hacking?" Niki asked.

"Any incompetent fool wouldn't have made it like Lyle ended up making it. He had to be desperate to do it that way."

"Someone told me that the present design saved crucial time and money. Do you see it the same way, or is there another reason?"

"The real reason is that Lyle Houston is an idiot. I'm glad it happened. Not that two people died, but someone took over a Sparrow and showed the world the danger."

"Are you capable of hacking into the Sparrow's navigational system?"

"In less time than this conversation is taking. I could crash every car that fool sells, and I might just do it."

CHAPTER EIGHTEEN

"ANYTHING INTERESTING?" Niki asked as she and Donna sat at their usual table at Linda's Chicken & Fish in Watson. The strawberry blonde detective ordered her usual meal; Cajun fried chicken livers, a cup of gumbo, fried dill pickles, and a cherry Dr. Pepper.

Donna ordered several items. Two triple cheeseburgers. An order of fried fish. Pastalaya. Fried okra. Niki marveled at how the hourglass blonde could eat so much and maintain her perfectly symmetrical figure.

"A lot of things," Donna answered. "Which one do you want to start with?"

"Let's start at the beginning. Let's start with Lyle Houston."

"For one, he's broke," the blonde said. "Lyle has every penny tied up in the company. The Eagle Autocar cash flow is negative. They aren't selling enough cars to pay the bills."

"Are you sure?" Niki asked. "I thought everyone in town was standing in line to get a Sparrow. How could they be losing money?"

"Expenses. The gross margin on each vehicle is less than the industry average, almost fifty percent less. Plus, he's giving away a maintenance warranty that makes his shop a liability rather than an asset."

"That would make a difference. I know for most dealerships, the shop is the real cash cow. If Lyle's is costing them money, then it sounds like a poor business plan to me."

"You nailed it," Donna said. "Unless sales triple, Lyle will run out of money. He'll either have to find another investor or someone to borrow a ton of money from."

"Or he may have to shut down, and that will be the end of Eagle Autocar. Is what Ralph said about the insurance policy true?"

"Lyle filed a claim with the insurance company this morning. He is asking for over two million dollars a day for as long as sales are suspended due to the accident."

Niki whistled. "That's a lot more than the bills."

Donna nodded.

"What did you find on Ralph Smith?" Niki asked.

"To say he is a disgruntled investor would be a major understatement. He has four lawsuits filed in the court so far."

"I guess he forgot to mention those to me," Niki chuckled. "Must have been an oversight on his part."

"Kinda like when a girl forgets to tell you she is pregnant. If she doesn't tell, she has a very good reason."

"What is he alleging in the civil suits?" Niki asked.

"Lyle Houston bamboozled him, although that's not the term that Ralph used. He is claiming fraud and deception on Lyle's part."

"Is there any basis for those claims?" Niki asked.

"Looks like it to me," Donna answered. "You said Lyle told you he put up most of the money because he had a lot more than Ralph. That turns out not to be true."

"Which part? Lyle having more money our Ralph not putting in much?"

"Both, actually. Ralph is worth thirty-five million, according to his accountant. At least, he was before he invested twenty million into Eagle Autocar stock for twenty percent of the ownership."

"That's a huge step. Investing over half your net worth in one project is a big risk. Not much diversity left when you do that."

"And it was backfiring on him. If there was ever to be a profit in Eagle Autocar, it was several years down the road."

"But at least, there was hope as long as Eagle Autocar was operating. With this design flaw exposed, I don't see how Ralph could ever recover any of his investment."

"Except that Ralph has an ace in the hole," Donna grinned as she cleaned the meat off a chicken wing.

"I'm all ears," Niki said. "What did you find?"

"Ralph has the right to the first refusal to buy the other eighty percent of the stock from Lyle Houston. If Lyle can't get the company going again, Ralph came to buy it for a song and a dance."

"But what would he do with a defunct car company?"

"Fix the problem. He has credibility since he warned Lyle several times the navigational system was vulnerable."

Niki nodded. "Then he could streamline expenses without any interference since he would own the whole company. I doubt it would take him long to recover his investment if he was the one running the company instead of Lyle."

Donna nodded her agreement.

"What about Joe Martin, the husband and father of the victims? Did you find anything about him out of the ordinary?"

Donna nodded, then took her time chewing a chunk of a triple cheeseburger before answering.

"I did. It seems that Joe Martin wasn't satisfied with the restraints of marriage."

"Do you mean he was having an affair? That will be totally opposite from the image he presented to me."

"I'd say it is. Old Joe is having a torrid tryst with a college freshman. Her name is Kristi O'Neill, and she's eighteen years old."

"Are you kidding?" Niki paused with a Cajun fried liver halfway to her mouth. "His daughter was sixteen, wasn't she?"

Donna nodded. "Young Kristi was good friends with Jamie. She was over at Jamie's house all the time."

"And old Joe couldn't stand the temptation. Going through a midlife crisis, he needed to verify his virility to himself and the world."

"That's the way it looks," Donna said. "You wouldn't believe some of the things they did. I'm still not sure some of them are physically possible."

"And you found this out how? Niki asked.

"Both of them love to relive the various acts. The more kinkier they were, the more they enjoyed talking about them. There are some porn magazines that wouldn't reprint their texts."

"Remind me to be careful what I text Dalton. I'd hate for my secrets with my fiancé to get out of to the public. You have to promise me you won't back into my emails or texts."

"You mean from now on?" Donna burst out laughing. "No, I have no interest in what you and the senator text back and forth. Be careful. The NSA records every single one of them."

"Anything else of interest about Joe Martin?" Niki asked.

"He raised the payouts on two insurance policies, one for his wife and the other for Jamie. That was only three months ago."

"Now that's convenient," Niki sighed. "What are the new payouts?"

"Two million for Lois and one million for Jamie. He is the sole beneficiary, and all the money is tax-free."

"Not bad. Three million net dollars. He and the eighteen-year-old will be able to party hardy for a long time on that much money."

"I think they've already started," Donna said. "Kristi O'Neill is driving a new Chevy Camaro courtesy of old Joe."

"And he said he was a computer engineer. I imagine he is more than capable of hacking into Eagle Autocar."

"In his sleep," Donna said. "And sex with an eighteen-year-old is enough motivation to make him do stupid things."

CHAPTER NINETEEN

"What about Rufus Pruitt? Is there any validity to his claim that Lyle stole the entire concept from him?" Niki asked.

"From what I've been able to dig up, Lyle lied to Rufus and screwed him big time. He wasn't delicate while doing it either."

"I don't get," Niki said. "Doesn't everyone have three lawyers and six paralegals these days? I would have assumed Rufus would have demanded an agreement in writing."

"He and Lyle had one, except Rufus didn't read the fine print. The contract stated all copyrights would be the property of Eagle Autocar, not the individual designers like Rufus."

"But that should have protected Rufus. Surely, he set it up so he would own a significant share of the company."

"He did," Donna nodded. "Except in one of the referenced footnotes, the contract stipulated Lyle could set the price and the number of stock shares to be sold. Rufus didn't have twenty million dollars."

"I see," Niki sighed. "So, at some point, Lyle went to Rufus and said, *sorry, you don't have the money to invest, so it will be impossible for you to be a part of our company.* I bet that conversation didn't go well for either of them."

"Not only that," Donna smiled. "But Rufus had already signed over all his drawings and schematics to Eagle Autocar. In essence, he donated all his work to Lyle without any compensation."

"Sounds like sufficient motivation to me," Niki said. "And I have no doubt about Rufus's capability to hack into the system."

"I bet he can make a Sparrow stand on its bumper," Donna laughed.

CHAPTER TWENTY

THE NEXT MORNING, Niki sat in front of the Tiger Plaza Apartments, number one twelve. That was the last address Donna could find for Kristi O'Neill. She found a few pictures of the coed on Facebook, and Niki swore she was looking at a young version of Angelina Jolie. Same black hair. Same wide forehead. Same high cheekbones. Same jutting chin. Same body.

When a girl came out of the apartment, Niki had no doubt she was Kristi O'Neill. Only Brad Pitt might have been able to tell the difference between the coed and the real version.

The private investigator watched the young girl get into a new yellow Camaro and speed out of the parking lot. Niki followed in her white Ford Explorer, blending in with the LSU traffic.

To Niki's disappointment, the Camaro headed toward the LSU campus. She followed and watched Kristi park in one of the lots assigned to students. Since Niki did not have a student parking pass, she had to find a visitor's lot with a meter. The meter accepted a credit card, and the fee kept churning until the SUV vacated the spot. The only good thing was the detective did not need to keep feeding the meter a steady diet of quarters.

She walked back toward the student lot and found a bench where she could keep an eye on the yellow Camaro. The wait turned out to be almost three hours. The coed was indeed still going to classes. Maybe, Niki thought, Joe Martin, and not yet revealed to her he had three million tax-free dollars.

The Camaro pulled out of the lot, turned left on College Drive, and then right on Interstate 12. Niki sighed. Kristi O'Neill was finally going in the direction the investigator desired. She was driving to Denham Springs.

Niki waited fifteen minutes in the SUV after arriving at Joe Martin's home. The yellow Camaro was hidden away in his garage, and Kristi O'Neill was inside the house. She had used her own key to gain entrance, a fact Niki photographed with her smartphone.

After the quarter of an hour passed, Niki drove up the driveway. Wasting no time, she jumped out of the SUV and rang the doorbell. When she did not get an immediate response, she rang it over and over again. Finally, Joe opened the door.

"Niki, what are you doing here?" He asked. "I'm sorry, but this isn't a good time for me. Can you come back this afternoon?"

He was wearing a robe, sandals, and not much else, even though it was approaching noon. He positioned his body in front of Niki so she could not see the interior of the home. She could not see Kristi.

"Joe, we need to talk. I think you'd better be straight with me rather than talk to the police. Let me in," Niki said.

"I'm sorry. I've already talked to the police. I told them the same thing I told you. I have nothing to add."

"It won't work, Joe. I know about the insurance upgrades for Lois and Jamie. I also know about Kristi. I bet she is back there in the bedroom wondering what is taking you so long."

The computer engineers countenance turned to ashen gray. At first, Niki thought that Joe's knees might buckle. Then, he recovered a little and stepped aside, allowing Niki to enter.

CHAPTER TWENTY-ONE

"YOU MIGHT AS WELL ASK Kristi to join us," she said, after having a seat. "It'll save me another conversation later."

Joe disappeared down the hall. Niki could hear the two lovers arguing in the master bedroom. Kristi's voice was the more shrill, and Niki figured the coed wanted no part of this mess.

Martin came down the hall alone. "She'll be a few minutes."

After another five minutes passed, Kristi appeared, tucking in the hem of her blouse into her jeans. The teenager glared at Niki, leaving no doubt about her feelings toward the investigator. The teenager plopped in a chair away from either of the other two, her hands clenched.

"Hi, Kristi. I'm Niki Dupre, and I'm investigating the death of Joe's wife and daughter. Do you mind answering a few questions?"

"I don't know nothing," the attractive girl said. "I never even knew the old witch or her daughter."

Joe winced at the crude reference to his wife from the teenager. This meeting had not gone well so far. He pivoted to stare at Kristi, who turned away and ignored him.

"That's okay. Just tell me what you know. How long has your affair been going on between the two of you?" Niki asked.

"It's not an affair," Joe said. "I met Kristi, and I'm in a vulnerable position. I guess I didn't use much common sense."

"Do what?" Kristi exploded. "Tell the truth, you old bastard."

"Are you saying the affair has been ongoing for a while?" Niki asked.

"You bet your sweet ass," Kristi bellowed. "He's been promising me for the last six months he was gonna leave the bitch."

"Is that true, Joe? Were you planning on divorcing Lois?"

"I–I–I might have mentioned something like that to Kristi, but I was just thinking about it. I wasn't really going to do it."

"You bastard," Kristi yelled. "You promised me. You said you would take me to Belize, and we could retire forever."

"Come on, Kristi. We were just talking," Joe pleaded with her.

"Come on, hell, I'm outta here."

The teenager burst out of the front door.

CHAPTER TWENTY-TWO

AFTER KRISTI LEFT, Joe stared at the space between his feet. The last thing he wanted to do was look at Niki.

"Well, Joe. It appears you lied to me. More than once."

"But it doesn't matter," the computer designer said. "Kristi was the whim of a middle-aged man. It was never going to be serious."

"Retiring on the beaches of Belize sounds serious to me," Niki said. "That sounds like a long–term promise to a young lady like Kristi."

"Look," Joe moved both palms to the side of his face. "Hasn't some guy ever promised you the moon to get what he really wanted?"

"Sure, but he wasn't twice my age, and his wife didn't die in a horrible car wreck. The men I dated weren't married in the first place."

"I admit it was a mistake," he sighed. "I doubt if Kristi will ever talk to me again after this meeting with you."

"Can you blame her?" Niki asked. "You just admitted in front of the girl you've been leading her on. How long has that been?"

"Almost a year," Joe admitted. "She used to come over with Jamie all the time. I used to tease her about what I wanted to do with her just to be funny. It turned out to be serious."

"So, at the time, she was seventeen, and you were flirting with her like a high school senior. She fell for all of it."

Joe nodded. "That's about the size of it. One day Kristi came over when Jamie wasn't here. We ended up in the bed together."

"And you never decided to make a mature decision to end it? Do you realize how that will make you look in this case?"

"Hey, I'm not the only man who ever dreamed of an affair with an attractive teenager. My dreams happened to come true."

"And your wife dies in a terrific crash along with your daughter, which makes you free as a bird. To boot, you'll have three million tax-free dollars to take Kristi to Belize."

CHAPTER TWENTY-THREE

"LYLE, you didn't tell me the whole truth," Niki said.

She and the owner of the Eagle Autocar sat in his office at the automobile manufacturing complex. She had only been there for two minutes, and he was already on a second cigarette.

"What are you talking about?" Lyle paced behind his desk. "I told you everything I know. There is nothing else to say."

"What about your insurance policy?" Niki asked. "Did you forget to tell me it will pay you over two million dollars a day until Eagle Autocar is back up in regular business?"

"That's because I haven't even thought about it," Lyle said. "I don't know if it would be applicable in this case, anyway."

"If you haven't thought about it, who filed the claim with the insurance company yesterday? I can show you a copy of it if you wish."

"How do you –? That's a private document. It's not available to the public. I ought to fire your ass right now."

"Doesn't matter. You can't fire me. I guess you didn't read the contract you signed. I will be involved until I find out who killed Lois and Jamie Martin."

"Okay. Okay." He threw up both hands, then lit another cigarette. "I remembered it yesterday. I had to file the claim to keep the company viable. Without that cash flow, we'll be out of business."

"Isn't Eagle Autocar starving for cash?" Niki asked. "Your company is close to being out of business, anyway."

"We are going through a period of negative cash flow. But a lot of businesses go through the same thing and survive."

"This windfall of new money makes it a lot easier. Your salesmen don't cost you anything right now, so you're probably making a nice profit off the insurance."

"But, our reputation is soiled." Lyle stopped pacing and stared at Niki. "Do you have any idea what that really means?"

"Yeah," Niki held his stare. "You want to blame it on one bad computer chip that went haywire, and you will implement a new testing procedure on all future chips you use in Sparrows."

Lyle dropped this gaze so fast Niki knew she had hit home with the theory. That plan was probably in front of the image-makers Eagle Autocar would have on retainer.

"Is there anything else you forgot to tell me?" Niki asked.

"Ralph Smith. I didn't tell you about a conversation we had last week. I guess I had put it out of my mind."

"Tell me about it and try to stick to the truth this time."

"He came by the office last Thursday, two days before Lois and Jamie Martin were killed. He wanted to buy me out." Lyle said.

"How much did he offer? Evidently, it wasn't enough."

"You're absolutely right. He didn't offer me anything. He offered to take it from me and catch up all the bills."

"So you would have walked away with nothing? Is that it?"

Lyle nodded. "I had to send him the financials since he is part owner. He knew our cash flow was suffering."

"And he wanted to kick you while you were down because you misled him about the money you put up."

Lyle plopped in his chair, suddenly tired. He lit another cigarette and took a long, slow drag. "I might not have told him the exact truth, but I never lied to him."

"Earth to Lyle. Not exactly telling the truth is the same as lying. There is no difference between the two."

"But I just left out some facts. That doesn't mean anything. He had the duty to do this own due diligence. Not me." Lyle said.

"How would he do a proper due diligence review if you were hiding facts like the total amount you invested?" Niki asked.

"It's still his responsibility, not mine. Anyway, I turned him down and tossed him out of my office," Lyle said, rising again.

"I guess that was difficult. After all, Ralph is younger and in better shape. I have a hard time visualizing you tossing him out."

"Okay, I threatened to call the police if he didn't leave. Then the stupid bastard tried to threaten me."

"What did he tell you that was so stupid?" Niki asked.

"He told me I was making a huge mistake. He said before he was finished, I would be begging him to take Eagle Autocar from me."

CHAPTER TWENTY-FOUR

BEFORE NIKI LEFT THE OFFICE, Lyle lit up another cigarette. Cancer from secondhand smoke became a reality. She saw Dennis Walker coming down the hallway.

"Hey, how are you doing today?" She asked the programmer.

"Fine, Miss Dupre. Where is Donna? She's something special," he said.

"She's back slaving at the office. I have to leave her there sometimes, or men won't ever pay attention to me," she laughed.

"Oh, I don't believe that, Miss Dupre. You're very attractive also, but it's just that Donna is so–so–unusual," he blushed.

"Don't worry," Niki put a hand on his shoulder. "I know I don't have the same features as Donna. Heck, nobody does. God didn't give me the same curves he gave my friend."

"It's okay," Dennis said. "What brings you here today?"

"Trying to get to the bottom of the Sparrow going berserk," the strawberry blonde said. "Do you have any ideas on the subject?"

"I'm not paid to solve that kind of problem. I've got my hands for coming up with a patch to build a firewall to the chip."

"I bet that won't be easy," Niki said. "How's it coming?"

"Not too good," Dennis admitted. "It's going to take a while. It's a good thing Lyle has the insurance policy that will kick in."

"You know about that?" Niki stopped walking. "I thought it was a big secret."

"In a company the size of Eagle Autocar, there aren't any secrets. All of us in programming were worried about losing our jobs."

"It shouldn't be hard for any of you to find another job," Niki said. "There is a huge demand for computer programmers."

"Not for those of us who come from failed projects," Dennis said. "If Eagle Autocar would have gone under, it would be a failed project."

"But that was because Lyle didn't want to spend the time and money create a fix? How could anyone blame you?"

"That's how it works in our industry. People aren't concerned about excuses. They only want to know about the end results."

CHAPTER TWENTY-FIVE

RALPH SMITH WAS NOT surprised to see the long-legged detective again. He met her at his door as though he was expecting Niki.

"What brings you back to my humble abode?" He asked after the two settled in his den. "May I get you a drink?"

"No, thank you," Niki answered. "I came back because I'm getting only half-truths in answers to my questions. I believe you are one of those who left out some very important information."

"I can't imagine anything of import I omitted," Ralph said.

"How about your attempt to buy out Lyle Houston? Did you offer to take Eagle Autocar from him for nothing?" Niki asked.

"I see you've been doing your job," Ralph smiled. "I was willing to give him all he deserved. That meant not one cent."

"Why didn't you tell me that before?"

"Because you didn't ask. I only answered specific questions, and you didn't ask that one. Maybe you should phrase your questions differently."

"All right. What did you mean when you told Lyle you weren't through? That he would beg you to take Eagle Autocar off his hands?"

For the first time, Ralph became noticeably uncomfortable. His eyes flitted right and left. He squirmed on the comfortable chair. His hands kept moving aimlessly all over the place.

"I didn't mean anything by. It was an idle threat," he said.

"It doesn't sound too idle in retrospect," Niki said. "Two days after you uttered those words, two people were killed in a wreck."

"You can't believe I had anything to do with that," Ralph said.

"Why not? You have the motive. You have the means. You probably know the Sparrow system as good as the programmers."

"Not really," Ralph tried to laugh. It didn't come off as real. "I'm not good at programming. I'm more of an idea kind of guy."

"Then you would have been at the mercy of Dennis Walker and the other lab guys for the company to succeed. Pardon my cynicism, but I don't believe you would put yourself in that situation."

"I–uh, I had a plan to modify the situation. I would not have been totally at the mercy of the programmers."

"So, how would you keep that from happening?" Niki asked.

"I'd rather not tell you that," Ralph said. "There is no reason to include anyone else in this mess right now."

"That's okay," Niki said. "I can draw my own conclusions."

CHAPTER TWENTY-SIX

"Rufus, you didn't tell me the whole truth," Niki said. "That seems to be a pattern in this whole thing."

The entrepreneur who came up with the concept of the electric Sparrow looked at the detective with disdain. "I'm not in the habit of telling my business to the public. Those that do find out they don't have any business to talk about."

"It still makes my job harder," the strawberry blonde said. "It would be a lot easier if you were more forthcoming."

"Your ease is not my concern. If you came here to cry on my shoulder, you can leave now. I have no time for babies."

"I'm not here to cry or complain," Niki said. "I'm here only to get someone to tell me the truth for a change."

"I told you the truth. Now, either get to your point or get the hell out of my office. I'm a busy person," Rufus snarled.

"I won't take up much of your precious time. Why didn't you tell me Ralph asked you to go into partnership with him after he bought Eagle Autocar from Lyle Houston?"

"How did you come up with that goofball idea?" Rufus asked.

"From Ralph Smith. He didn't want to be dependent on the

programmers for the success of Eagle Autocar. That means he needed someone with more expertise than them. That means you."

"I doubt if Ralph voluntarily gave up that information. You must have an unusual technique to get him to talk."

Niki didn't want to admit she was guessing. It was a guess based on the fact, but it was still a gas. She breathed a sigh of relief when Rufus confirmed her idea.

"How big would your percentage have been?" Niki asked.

"Forty percent," Rufus replied. "I'm surprised Ralph didn't tell you."

"He was a bit upset by the time I left," Niki said "I didn't get to ask him everything I wanted."

"Is that how I make you leave?" Rufus smiled. "Do I need to throw a fit so you won't ask more questions?"

"If I leave, it means only that I'll come back if necessary."

"It wasn't me," Rufus said. "Yes, I wanted for the company because it was my idea and my design. Lyle should never have stolen it from me and taken it for himself."

"You know that sounds like a motive for murder," Niki said. "And you certainly have the expertise to pull it off."

"If I were going to kill anyone, I wouldn't have selected two innocent clients," Rufus said. "I would have killed Lyle Houston."

"Isn't that what this did? Figuratively, if not literally. He no longer has a reputable company, and he is strapped for cash."

"I can't say I feel sorry for Lyle. He's a poor excuse for a human being. He deserves to suffer a long, long time."

CHAPTER TWENTY-SEVEN

After a long day, Niki needed a respite. For the strawberry blonde, that meant Cajun fried chicken livers at Linda's. She and Donna took their familiar seats in the far back corner.

Both ordered their usual meals. Niki's included the livers with dill pickles, gumbo, and a cherry Dr. Pepper. Donna ordered parts of pages one, two, and three of the menu board. Whatever was happening in the case was not affecting her appetite.

"I saw your new boyfriend," Niki teased. "He asked about you."

"New boyfriend?" Donna squinted until she came up with the name. "You mean Dennis Walker? How is he doing?"

"Relieved," Niki said. "All the programmers were concerned about Eagle Autocar closing. Now with the insurance kicking in, they don't have to fear that happening for a while."

"I'm glad," Donna beamed as only she could. "He is such a sweet person. I don't meet many people like him in our business."

"Sounds like a relationship in the budding. At least, you both love computers. You'll have that much in common."

"I don't know," Donna shrugged. "He's really nice, but he's a nerd. I kind of like a more manly man. Know what I mean?"

"I do," Niki sighed. "But most macho men tend to let us down. Before I met Dalton, I was madly in love with one. That ended up with him trying to kill me."

"I know, but—hold on. I just got a message," Donna said.

Niki watched her young friend's face form a puzzle. After the youngster finished reading the text, she raised her brows.

"It's bad," the hourglass blonde said. "Dennis should be concerned again. The insurance company just denied Lyle's claim."

CHAPTER TWENTY-EIGHT

LYLE RECEIVED the notification of denial at the same time as Donna. He was also puzzled, along with enraged and terrified. He had been counting on the money for his survival. He yanked up the phone to call his agent.

"Ben," he yelled into the phone. "What the hell is going on? How in the world could you assholes deny my claim?"

"Calm down," the insurance agent said. "We just can't throw money at Eagle Autocar because of one small tough period.

"You had no problem taking the premium money," Lyle shouted. "Now, you aren't willing to pony up."

"Our board doesn't agree one incident is a showstopper. All automobile companies have a lemon or two that causes embarrassment. None of them went out of business right away."

"But we're a startup," Lyle screamed. "We don't have an adequate stash of reserve cash to make it through this."

"I'm sorry, Lyle. I can send an appeal to the board, but I wouldn't get my hopes up if I were you. In my eight years here, I have never seen those guys reverse themselves. They won't do it now."

"But I'll be out of business within a month. We were already hurting, and now we're plumb out of customers. Tell me how I'm supposed to keep my doors open."

"I wish I could help you," the agent said. "If another incident happens, the board may take a different look at it."

Lyle slammed the phone down, only to have it ringing almost immediately. Without thinking, the owner picked it up.

"Hello," he said gruffly; his mood was still sour. It did not improve.

"Hello, Lyle. This is Ralph. I got the same notice as you."

"I should have known that you would call to gloat. Don't forget your twenty percent will suffer the same fate as mine."

"Not if you decide to sell the company to me," Ralph said.

"Sell it to you are give it to you? The last offer you made, if you can call it an offer, was to pay me nothing."

"You have to admit," Ralph said. "Eagle Autocar isn't worth a lot right now. Don't you want to see it survive?"

"Not without me," Lyle yelled into the phone. "There ain't no way I'm going to let you steal my company from me."

"You don't have a company. You won't stay in business for six more weeks. You'll have a liquidation sale."

"That's better than giving it to you for nothing," Lyle said.

"How about I throw in a million for you?" Ralph asked. "Could that alter your position in the least?"

"Not one damn bit," Lyle shouted and slammed the phone down.

CHAPTER TWENTY-NINE

JOE MARTIN HAD no idea about Lyle Houston's insurance policy. All he knew was that his world had fallen apart. His wife and daughter were dead. His young girlfriend wasn't speaking to him. And to top it off, the best private investigator in Louisiana thought he was a murderer.

He tried to call Kristi half a dozen times. Each time, the call went directly to her voicemail. His last was blocked. The voicemail box was full. He blamed Niki Dupre. Until the private investigator interfered, his relationship with Kristi was fabulous. He had a little trouble keeping up with the new vocalists she thought were hot. He did not want to go to the single bars she enjoyed. But the sex was fabulous.

But now the sex was gone, and Joe was not sure when, or if, it would never return. He had risked a lot for the experience. He risked his marriage for too long. He risked alienating his daughter. She would not have understood an affair with her best friend and her dad. But his relationship with his wife and daughter had stayed hidden until they died.

He was free. No responsibility as a husband. No responsibility as a father. Plus, the insurance company had already approved the payments totaling three million dollars. He was free and rich. With absolutely nowhere to go.

CHAPTER THIRTY

RUFUS PRUITT WAS NOT sure what Richard Smith expected from him. The conversation had been going on for ten minutes, and so far, had very little substance.

"Didn't you expect Lyle to turn you down?" Rufus asked.

"Not really," Ralph replied. "I thought he might see the light. I guess he is so blinded by his pride and ego he can't see things for what they really are."

"That doesn't surprise me," Rufus said. "Lyle was never a great programmer. He was awful. But his ego wouldn't let him admit he needed me beyond the initial concepts."

"He has hired a full staff of programmers," Ralph replied. "That's one of his problems. He'll have to figure out some way to pay those guys, or he'll lose them."

"I don't see how he'll pay them," Rufus said. "Nobody wants to buy a Sparrow until they know what caused the crash."

"That won't happen unless Lyle admits someone hacked into his navigational system. That will be pure suicide to show the world how vulnerable it is."

"I don't think he has a choice," Rufus said. "I don't know of anything else he can do."

"He can sell Eagle Autocar to us," Ralph said.

"It sounds like that's out of the question," Rufus replied. "Maybe he needs for the other shoe to drop."

CHAPTER THIRTY-ONE

JOHN CASEY WAS ELATED. He was able to buy a new Sparrow for a ridiculously low price. When he arrived at the showroom, no salesman rushed to greet him. He wandered around, looking at the different models on the floor for ten minutes before he saw movement.

It was Lyle Houston, the owner. John recognized him from the numerous photos in the media. At first, the customer thought he was about to be told to leave. Instead, Lyle greeted him like a long–lost cousin. The owner practically begged him to buy a Sparrow.

In the end, John offered an insultingly low price, one he feared would offend the famous owner. Instead, Lyle eagerly accepted it and had the car ready to travel in less than half an hour.

Now, the proud new owner steered his silver Sparrow back down Airline Highway toward Gonzalez. Once he passed Sherwood Forest, the road opened up, allowing him to test the powerful electric engine.

To his surprise, the Sparrow responded with more power than he expected. It jumped up to seventy miles an hour. Then eighty. Then ninety.

John took his foot off the pedal and hit the brakes. He did not want to crash the car on its first drive. Now that he knew the little car had that kind of acceleration, John was satisfied.

But the Sparrow did not slow down. Instead, it continued to increase in speed. Ninety-five. One hundred. One hundred five miles per hour. He could no longer steer. The auto–feature took over, and the Sparrow navigated itself. But not for long.

At a sharp curve, the Sparrow failed to maneuver fast enough. The small automobile left the road, crossed the shoulder, and sailed through the air. When the electric car hit the live oak tree, it crushed like a tin can.

CHAPTER THIRTY-TWO

Niki and Donna stared at the wreckage. There was no way the driver could have survived. In that mingle of metal, a sardine would have been crushed.

Local Sheriff's deputies shared the same thoughts. Instead of calling for the Jaws of Life, they summoned the corners office. The only question was how many pieces into which the body had been broken. The mood of the scene was between sober and dire.

"He must've went loco," one deputy came up to the investigators. "We've got a couple of witnesses that said he went by them like a train going by a hobo. They said he had to be going more than a hundred."

"Could they tell if he was steering or the car was?"

"Huh?" The deputy did not catch on it first. "Oh, you mean this is one of those self–striving gizmos. I'll be sure to put that in my report. Don't seem like they're too safe."

"This is the second incident in less than a week," Niki said. "The other one killed a mother and daughter."

"Oh, yeah. I recall that now," the deputy said, "You know, that one was going more than a hundred according to the reports. Do you reckon there is some sort of connection?"

"I know there is," Niki said. "Don't write this up as an accident. It was murder, pure and simple."

"How will you prove it?" Donna asked.

"I don't know yet, but the killer crossed the line. He went one step too far."

CHAPTER THIRTY-THREE

"JOE, I didn't hear you come in," Niki said.

"You weren't meant to. I'm not just a computer programmer, I'm a Special Forces assassin in the Army. I've snuck up on more stupid people than you can count."

"Did you talk to all of them before you killed them?" Niki asked as she moved to her right. As soon as her body was between Martin and Donna, the private investigator stopped.

"Nope, you're the first. The rest of them were butchers, and they faced death every day. I didn't offer any explanation to them."

"And you must feel like you owe me one," Niki said.

"I think that's only fair. The soldiers know why they have to die. They are fighting Americans. But you might not know."

"I think I have a pretty good idea. You lost the lust of your life, and you've got to blame someone. Since I am handy, you chose me. That's pretty narrow-minded."

"Not in my shoes, Niki. You've ruined my life, and now I'm here to take yours. Unfortunately, I'll have to kill Miss Cross. Can't leave any witnesses, you know."

Niki put her left hand behind her back. She held out three fingers and pointed to the floor. Then she showed her hand again to Joe to prove it was empty.

Three–two–one. Both women exploded into motion. Donna dropped straight down behind the sofa hidden from Joe. Niki somersaulted right at the Special Forces soldier.

It was the last move Joe expected. All of his other victims who had any chance had tried to flee or gain cover. The six pillows on the front side of the piece of furniture stopped the first projectile from hitting Donna. Joe tried to adjust the aim at the blur coming directly at him. He pulled the trigger one more time. This time, the bullet dug into the carpet between Joe and the sofa. Before he could adjust his aim, Niki's foot crashed into his rib cage. He flew back, landing on his back in the kitchen.

Before the soldier could recover, Niki kicked the Ruger pistol out of his hand, sending it ricocheting off of the cabinets next to the kitchen sink. Then, he was at the mercy of the Kempo six-degree black belt. It turned out to be no contest. By the time Niki finished, Joe was out cold.

CHAPTER THIRTY-FOUR

Donna and Niki watched the deputies and EMTs haul off Joe's unconscious body. In the thirty-minute interval, the assassin had shown no signs of awareness. Both deputies and the medical technicians commented about the thorough beating Niki had perpetrated upon the intruder.

"Do you think you overdid it a bit?" Donna chuckled.

"Not at all. He came here with the intent of killing us. In case some silly judge lets him out on bail, I wanted to dissuade him of that notion."

"I think you did more than that," Donna laughed. "I doubt if old Joe will remember his name for the foreseeable future."

"I hope not," Niki replied. "And I hope he doesn't remember our names until he's behind bars for good."

"Gonna be tough in the spend those three million dollars at Angola. I think they have a limit on how much the inmates can buy from the commissary every month. It'll take him six lifetimes to spend that kind of money."

"I hope he spends every dime on an expensive, worthless lawyer.

Those sleazebags will know everything he has in his account, and they'll drain it all dry."

"I can't believe that Joe was Special Forces," Donna said.

"If he was, my bet is he was a communications technician. He made up all of that about being an assassin. The closest he came to combat was to mop up the injured and the laggards."

"What makes you come to that conclusion?" Donna asked.

"He was aiming the pistol at my head. Any true assassin would have aimed it at my body. Center mass makes a bigger target than a moving head. He didn't know that."

"I was too scared to notice," Donna admitted. "But, I guess that solves our problem for us."

"Which one is that?" Niki looked at her friend.

"It's obvious Joe killed his family. Then when you are about to prove it, he went off the deep end. I don't see any other explanation for what he tried to do today."

"It's call sex," Niki laughed. "We messed up his relationship with his teenage lover, and he didn't care for that a little bit."

"But you still think Joe did it, don't you?" Donna asked.

"No, I don't," replied Niki. "But now, I know who did."

"Who is it?"

"Someone with a lot to lose. I need you to go with me and support whatever I say."

CHAPTER THIRTY-FIVE

NIKI AND DONNA walked into the abandoned showroom at the Eagle Autocar complex. There was no one in sight. The pair walked down the hallway and heard Lyle yelling into the phone at the insurance company agent.

To Donna's surprise, they continued walking past the door. They went all the way to the lab.

"Hey, Dennis," Donna beamed, when she saw her new friend.

"Uh–hey–what are you doing here?" The programmer asked.

"Niki knows who is responsible for hacking into the chips and killing those people," Donna answered.

"She does?" The color drained from Walker's face.

"Yes, I do," Niki answered. "I came here to give you a chance to turn yourself in before we gather the concrete evidence."

"What–what evidence?" He stammered.

"You've seen Donna's capabilities. The East Baton Rouge Sheriff's Department has agreed to let her examine the chip. She'll be able to trace the intervention directly to you."

"Can you really do that?" Dennis asked Donna.

"Sure," the hourglass blonde answered, though she was not at all certain it was a possibility.

Dennis turned slowly back to his desk. When he pivoted back around, he was holding a small pistol.

"How did you figure it out?" He asked Niki while pointing the pistol between her eyes.

"Simply the process of elimination," Niki replied. "Ralph and Rufus get hurt if the insurance kicks in. Then Lyle won't have to give Eagle Autocar to them. The last thing they wanted was another fatality."

"So that would point the finger at Lyle," Dennis said.

"You and I both know that Lyle is not a programmer. He couldn't hack into his own system if he had to."

"What about the husband, the Martin guy?"

"He's already tried to get even with me in a much more direct way. So that leaves you. You were afraid your career was going down the toilet with Eagle Autocar."

"I'm sorry you came to that conclusion," Dennis said. "Now, I'll have to kill both of you."

"You can't, Dennis," Niki said. "You might be able to pull the trigger on me, but there is no way you can shoot Donna. She has been too kind to you."

Dennis looked at Donna and whimpered like he was a small puppy. His eyes filled with affection, not hate.

Niki did not see the affection. As soon as Dennis focused on her friend, the detective's foot exploded. The impact with Walker's forearm sent the small pistol flying toward the tall ceiling. Dennis grabbed his broken arm and sank to his knees.

He looked up at Donna.

"She was right. There is no way I could've shot you."

Dear reader,

We hope you enjoyed reading *Murder on Autopilot*. Please take a moment to leave a review, even if it's a short one. Your opinion is important to us.

Discover more books by Jim Riley at

https://www.nextchapter.pub/authors/jim-riley

Want to know when one of our books is free or discounted? Join the newsletter at

http://eepurl.com/bqqB3H

Best regards,

Jim Riley and the Next Chapter Team